to Yoko

First published in Great Britain in 2009 by Andersen Press Ltd.,

20 Vauxhall Bridge Road, London SW1V 2SA.

Published in Australia by Random House Australia Pty.,

Level 3, 100 Pacific Highway, North Sydney, NSW 2060.

Copyright © David Lucas, 2009.

The rights of David Lucas to be identified as the author and illustrator

of this work have been asserted by him in accordance with

the Copyright, Designs and Patents Act, 1988.

All rights reserved.

Colour separated in Switzerland by Photolitho AG, Zürich.

Printed and bound in Singapore by Tien Wah Press.

10 9 8 7 6 5 4 3 2 1

British Library Cataloguing in Publication Data available.

ISBN 978 1 84270 636 7

Cake Girl

David Lucas

ANDERSEN PRESS

The Witch was alone
on her birthday . . . *again!*

So she baked
a Cake Girl.

And told her to sing
'Happy Birthday'.

And dance.

And smile.

And make her laugh.

And do all the housework . . .

"And then," said the Witch,
"I'll eat you."

HAPPY BIRTHDAY TO ME

"What shall I do?"
wondered Cake Girl.

She looked up.
"I expect you're having
a big birthday party?"
she said.

"Party?"
said the Witch,
"I'm not having a party."

Her hat spun round
and she turned away.

"No one likes me," she said.

"But why don't you use MAGIC
to make people like you?" said Cake Girl.

"I made you," said the Witch,
"and you don't like me."

"But you're not nice to me,"
said Cake Girl.

"*Hmmm . . .*"
The Witch was thinking.
Her hat spun round at great speed.

"Do you mean that
if I were nice to you,
that then you'd like me?"

"Yes," said Cake Girl.
"Promise?" said the Witch.
"*Yes,*" said Cake Girl.

"But I don't know
how to be nice,"
said the Witch.

"Perhaps you could help me?" said Cake Girl.
"Oh yes! That's easy!" said the Witch, and snapped her fingers —
the housework was done in a flash.

"And perhaps . . ."
said Cake Girl,
a little nervously,

"you don't have
to eat me?"

"*Hmmm . . .*" said the Witch.

"Difficult. You *do* look delicious . . ."

She stroked her chin.

"Well, I suppose I could have a
bit of bread and butter instead."

"And perhaps," said Cake Girl, feeling braver now,
"you could sing *me* a song?"
"*Oho!*" said the Witch. "Me? Sing?"

She
did
her
best.

"And dance!"
said Cake Girl
happily.

"And smile!"

"And make me
laugh!"

"And do MAGIC tricks!"
said Cake Girl,
clapping her soft,
marzipan hands.

"Oh, I love doing magic tricks!"
said the Witch.

And she turned herself
into a great big fancy cake —
and laughed and laughed
until she nearly crumbled to bits.

"I can turn myself into
anything!" she said.

"And you too, if you like!"
said the Witch, "I can turn
you into anything.
Anything at all!"

"A princess!" said Cake Girl.
And suddenly she was a princess,
and the Witch was a splendidly
wicked-looking queen.

"Or a firework!" said Cake Girl —
and they shot off into the sky
with a bang.

They fluttered back down as birds.

And then the Witch showed Cake Girl
(who wasn't made of cake any more)
how to work magic,
and turn herself into
whatever she liked.

And when they were tired
the Witch turned into
a big comfortable armchair
and Cake Girl turned into a cat.

It was the best birthday
either of them had ever had.